Thoughts

By
Earvin P Eugene

Table Of Contents

By Earvin Eugene

In the past, maybe two or three decades ago lived a man of art, a meaningful and articulate character of creation, who before this story developed had made a craft of unworldly attraction than any artwork. He had left his studio to the care of a friend, removed his fine instruments and there was a view of a blank canvas. The man was able to marry a pretty lady. In these times life imitated art. The artist curated a world of love and passion with a great design. He allowed his thoughts to overcome him on occasion. This was the essence of fine art. Axel had qualities of good performance and demonstration. His art was his life. The only competition was for his beautiful young wife. The dilemma was combining the two for an unhealthy intimacy.

The marriage between the love of art and his wife was truly outstanding. One day, Axel stared at his wife with trouble. An issue was escalating.

He said, Ariel, "has it never occurred to you that you possess many freckles. It is present on your cheeks, your breasts, your body. Would you ever conceal them?"

"No, I never thought much of it", she said with a smile. She was curious. "Honestly, many people tell me of their cuteness, so I assume it to be pleasing."

"Maybe it is for some", replied her husband; "but you are perfect by every other regard. No, my love Ariel, it is not for others to decide whether they are blemishes or marks of beauty, it is perceived to me as the only presentation you have of imperfection."

"How could you say such a thing?" cried Ariel, feeling hurt; she was mad, and then starting to shed tears. "Why did you marry me if that is the case? To be so vain, you cannot love what you dislike."

To think about this conversation, it must be mentioned that her freckles were on complete display. There was an array of flecks that meshed with the texture and substance of her skin. Many men observed this and believed it appreciated her value. It was interesting and defining. Axel, himself did not ponder about it before.

He found this one flaw rising. It started to become intolerable for him. It was considered a mistake or error to him. When considering pure aesthetic art, it was a blunder. It is the order of humanity to seek symmetry and clearness. The lack of perfection brought him torment and pain. It would be the utmost achievement to create an image of perfect beauty of his wife. He never attempted to do it before. It could be his greatest work. Ariel's soul was so delightful that he believed he could forget this. He tried. He failed to overcome this. It became an obsession. Axel was on the pursuit for excellence.

Even in their greatest moments, without realizing it he would focus on her freckles. In the morning, Axel would lay his eyes on his wife and noticed the symbol of stain. When they ate meals together, walked in the park, watched a movie, he shyly glanced at her and focused on her specks.

One evening when things were quiet, she discussed the idea. Ariel said, "Are you thinking about my freckles?" She said this with a fake smile and slight disdain. He responded, "At no fault of my own, I question it at times. My love, Ariel, I wish to draw you. I want to depict the ultimate beauty you possess. If it is to be my masterpiece, should I share you in a lesser light?" She replied, "If there is a possibility to make things better, let us proceed. If this is going to grow to an even bigger problem, we must solve it. It seems my freckles are not so pronounced. You have great skill. If you were to cater to me and display me in your art, then let us make it as perfect as it can be. Are you capable of creating work that will give me peace?"

Axel stated, "Ariel, my lovely wife, I have a plan. You have brought me closer to my art. I have decided to fix this mishap. It will be my greatest achievement to relinquish what human nature has formed and relay it to a better work. Artists in the past have created close to perfection in a certain circumstance. In my position, your true appearance will be established and be magnificent to see.

Ariel responded, "It is agreed! She reluctantly smiled. Now we can move on. You will find me as you always have." Her husband gave her a grand kiss avoiding her freckles.

A few days later, Axel showed his wife of a strategy that he formulated. In his studio, the originator studied techniques from across the world. Concepts of nature and society were considered. Thoughts of international best kept secrets on profound art were noted. The perceptions of beauty, exhibition, and arrangements were read. He satisfied himself of the reactions of different colors and tones. Every object within the workshop had its value and place. To the inexperienced eye it appeared to render a spectacle.

Both of them alongside a team shared the area. Axel seemed to be glad. Ariel was overwhelmed. The group mentioned, "I do not see the reason to not depict her freckles." Your wife is astonishing. Axel ignored the suggestions. He comforted his wife illustrating to her various paintings and images. He described the similar layout he would use in drawing her. Axel reminded her of her uniqueness. The studio was set up with calming music and dignified lighting. There was an aura of acceptance.

He provided his wife with a formula. He described it as some sort of medicine. Something to calm the nerves. Soon, she possessed a certain vibrant quality. Axel quickly started to work. There was a sensation that time is of the essence. The squad mumbled and talked in a suspicious manner. They applied her with make-up. She was more attractive than ever before.

Axel performed to his best attributes. He worked vigorously. Axel stared at Ariel with such passion. He placed soft strokes on the canvas. Axel utilized a complete spectrum of colors. Ariel began to sweat. She believed it was due to stress. She voiced her concerns. Axel disregarded her. He needed to keep working. It was blind passion. In a few moments, Ariel's eyes turned red and she felt nauseous. Again, she made a statement. Axel said, "Please my love be still." The team patiently viewed her from afar. Taking photos of her. Writing notes. Adjusting the lights and creating a serene environment. The atmosphere emulated fine art itself. It was time! Axel exclaimed. "Yes!" He was finished. First, he showed his personal curators his artwork. They applauded with joy. They clapped and gave their expert remarks. One mentioned, "That is perfect, do not change a thing." At last, he went to show his greatest admirer, Ariel of the completed work. At this point she was terribly ill. She looked at the painting and cried. Within seconds she left us…

The Perfect Bar

By Earvin Eugene

There was an old man who visited this certain clean and standard bar. He frequented the café often. It was a quaint location. Customers could buy coffee, tea, typical liquors, and appropriate snacks. The senior appeared to always be tipsy. He was a mature man. You could tell that he labored most of his life. Now, he is quiet and enjoying the fruits of his labor. He seems jaded and slightly decrepit. He was a popular aged man in a small city. It was late at night and few people attended this bar. It could be full of commotion earlier in the evening but at this hour, it was the old man and a few customers. The other customers were green to this atmosphere. The aged man was a veteran in comparison.

The waiter was satisfying a customer, he mentioned, "I know that old man. Didn't you hear he tried to kill himself last month. And that was not the first time!"

The waiter, replied, "Him? He is successful. He comes to this bar almost every night."

The customer, stated, "It is a sad story. Just repeating what I heard is depressing."

The waiter, asked, "Why? What happened?"

The customer, mentioned, "It is not for me to say. I heard he is in agony for the loss of his late wife. Also, the stress of receiving such amount of money with no lover over a long period of time could be overwhelming. I do not know how he became rich. Do you?"

The waiter was in disbelief. He quickly, stated, "No!" He had to cut the conversation short and return to the staff."

The old man with weary eyes just finished his drink. He provided a quick glance at the waiter, but it appeared that he was just viewing the room.

One waiter conversed with another waiter, "It is long night. I want to go home. Did you hear, the old man attempted suicide?"

The other waiter, replied, "Why?" He was cut short as the old man raised his hand for another drink.

The old man, said, "I would like a whiskey, neat." The waiter followed the demand. He asked, "Why do you come here alone almost every night?" The old man, responded, "I have nowhere else to be."

The waiter returned to the other waiter. He stated, "He is useless!"

The other waiter, replied, "Relax, you do not what he is going through."

A young lady entered the bar. She sat beside the old man. She seemed concerned. There was a second of bickering and then the mature man reluctantly agreed.

The old man raised his hand once more. The waiter approached. The old man said, "I would like a whiskey, neat." The lady was discovered to be the man's daughter and detested. She stated, "That is enough." The old man said, "do not be a hassle." They quarreled and reconciled. The daughter unwillingly approved of one last drink.

The waiters discussed that the daughter was there when the father attempted suicide. At least that is what the rumor suggested. They felt sorry for the poor girl to be put in this position.

The waiters discussed that on one drunken night, the old man went into the pool in the backyard and attempted to drown himself. The daughter found him there silent in the water. She rescued him!

Now, the old man stumbled and left the bar with his daughter by his side…

THE END

By Earvin Eugene

Knowing that Mr. Miller was affected by panic attacks, a great deal of consideration was taken to break the bad news to him. Without much notice but with as much care as possible he was told of the possibility of his wife's death.

The message came from his brother, Victor, started by grim silence; a sad face and stressful demeanor presented negativity. One could tell the truth was burdensome. His wife's friend Cynthia was there, too, near him. It was her who had been on social media when information of the car crash was received, with Jessica Miller's name in bold letters on the list of "deceased". She double-checked Online. She saw it on several of her friends' posts. People were sharing it everywhere. She viewed the news repeatedly. It could be no hoax or cruel joke.

He did not hear the story as many females have in the way they spread the narrative. They were all in confusion. They could not accept the reality. Cynthia shed tears; she was distraught. She needed time alone. Everyone gave her much needed space.

There Mr. Miller stood, looking through the open window. He sat down thinking. He was tired. Mr. Miller tried to remain as calm as possible. His thoughts raced. His life was in turmoil. He believed he would never be at peace again.

He viewed outside and could see the trees, animals, and flowers. The spring breeze was relaxing. The moisture in the air was soothing as rain was in the forecast. In the street below a walker who was whistling. The sounds of nostalgic songs were playing by local stores. It reminded him of a better time. Without realizing he hummed the melody.

The sky was clear and lightly blue. The window was an escape from a sorrowful point of time inside. He sat with his head now at the bed. It was comfy. He did his best not to cry. It was shameful for a man at his age to shed tears. If he were a child, he would have innocence.

He was mature, with a somber face, stillness and clear. It was the appearance of a remainder of youth right before distinguished wrinkles would become present. At this moment there was a lackluster glare in her eyes, whose view was located away somewhere on one of those clouds in the sky. It was not a gaze of remorse, but rather indicated a mystery of clever thought.

There was something coming over him and he did not like the feeling. He could not put a finger on it. He did not know what to do. He was too clueless to recognize it. There was a shadow hanging over him. All the signs pointed to something ominous.

Now his chest felt strain and heat. He was realizing something important. Mr. Miller knew this was immoral, but he embraced it. He reached a glimmer of hope and happiness. His heartbeat fast. He said it aloud: "At last I am free!" The bad stare and the look of trouble that had followed it started from his eyes as he roamed the room. Soon his vision became concise and vibrant as he looked in the mirror. He was hot and heavy. He saw a new man.

He felt regretful joy. He knew that he would feel sorrow when the dreadful funeral occurred. To witness his beautiful and pleasant wife in such a horrid position would be terrible. Death of a loved one can never be good. He did not want to paint a portrait of her at her death bed. However, he removed himself from that bitter time.

It was selfish but he could live on his own accord. There would be no one to answer for during those coming years; he would experience "freedom". There would be no commitment for blind allegiance that men and women believe they have a right to impose upon each other. Who is to say whether it is good or bad but there is something to question in the lifestyle in which society imposed on marriage. At the time there was a sense of true liberation. There was no lying to the fact that he loved her most of the time. On many occasions he did not. Who cares? What is love? Shouldn't it include to feel alive. That is a strong emotion maybe even greater than love itself.

"I'm released!" He kept thinking.

Cynthia was nearby behind the closed door with her lips to the keyhold, asking for entrance. "Miller, open the door! Please; open the door--you will get sick. What is going on, Miller? C'mon open the door."

"Leave me alone. I am fine." No; he was smoking tobacco through that open window.

He pondered about the upcoming days. All the days of the seasons. Hot and cold days, times with perfect weather. And all those typical and new sorts of days that he would be independent. He hoped that life would be long and amazing. He decided to open the door and share life with friends and family. There was a sense of confidence. An unsure feeling of accomplishment. He shook his brother's hand. They went down the stairs. His environment was calm. Miller was relieved. Through the roller coaster of emotions, he believed he was done with that journey. He was exhausted.

There was a sound of the front door opening. It was his wife who entered, a little tired, calmly carrying her stuff. She was slightly disheveled and was in her work attire. She had been far from the scene of the accident and did not even know there had been one. She was bewildered by the shock in the house. She stood amazed at Mr. Miller's face.

When the ambulance arrived, they said he had a stroke.

He entered the bedroom to turn on the lights and close the window while the girl was still in bed and I noticed she was greatly sick. The fresh air was intended to improve her breathing and provide coolness. She was sweating with a fever, her eyes were weak, and she moved with soreness.

The father, stated, "What is wrong?"

The child, replied, "I do not feel well."

He, said, "You should not move so much, it is time to relax in bed."

The daughter, replied, "It is not so bad. I was tired of being in bed all day."

The father provided honey and tea for his eleven-year-old daughter in her room. He mentioned that he will be dressed at the kitchen. He wanted to prepare some medicine if his child's illness was to get worse.

In a few minutes, the daughter followed the father downstairs. She wanted to move to be alert and refreshed. It was of no use; she was still in agony.

The father showed disapproval to his child, he stated, "You should not be downstairs. It is better for you to be in bed."

She said, "I am okay."

The dad took the daughter's temperature. It was one hundred and one degrees, Fahrenheit.

The father provided medications to treat pain, fever, and cough. Ensuring it was in the right doses for her young age. The dad told his daughter, "The best remedy is rest and fluids." The daughter drank cold water with the medicine.

The dad and daughter returned to the bedroom. The father decided to watch a movie with the girl. It was a childish flick, that she usually enjoyed. In this moment, she did not pay any attention. She would switch between focus and confusion.

"How do you feel Emily?", I asked her

"I feel tired."

The father wanted to monitor the daughter and continue to watch the movie with her. When it was appropriate to provide the next dose of medicine, he hoped to see improvement.

He stated, "Emily, go to bed and I'll wake you up when it is time for medicine." She replied, "No, I want to watch the movie with you Dad."

It appeared she had cold sweats. Her movements still slow and painful. I provided her the medication at the proper time and left her with cold water.

Outside it was treacherous. Rainy and cold. It was wet and windy. The father thought today is not a good day.

Inside the residence, the girl wanted to be alone.

The father realized, her mind must be hazy, and she made statements of a headache earlier in the day. She was tossing and turning in bed. The dad checked her temperature. It was now, one hundred degrees. There was improvement!

The daughter did not believe it. She stated, "What's the point"

The father gave her some cold water. She said, "I will be sick forever!"

The father attempted to continue to view the movie with the girl. She mentioned, "one hundred degrees seems to be high." The dad explained her body is normally around ninety-eight degrees and in time her fever will drop from one hundred to ninety-eight. She replied, "I do not believe it!"

The dad said, "Trust me, Emily."

The father explained, "You have an infection, which is caused by germs. Your body naturally reacts to raise its temperature through a fever. At this higher body temperature, the germs can not properly live and are killed. During this fever, your body aches. As you return to normal and as the infection clears, everything will be better."

The daughter replied, "I think I get it."

The following day, the daughter was annoyed at little things and was more energetic. The father did what fathers do and cared for his child.

THE END

By Earvin Eugene

Sad! Very weary. Worrisome and fearful. I feel lost; will you say that I am wrong? Should I not feel this way. The ailment had made me self-conscious, no longer dramatized, but self-aware. There was a clever mix between thought and physical perceptions. Somehow, I saw things clear for the first time. Heard my surroundings with clarity. Felt true pain. Tasted a bitterness that life always provides. Smelled a nasty and deadly aroma. How could this be a disease? When I am relaxed in understanding the torment of life. I can share this accurate account.

The first moment I realized this narrative, it was profound. It bothered me plenty. I could not forget it. There was no emotion as I visited this familiar place. I deeply cared for these people. They were family, friends, colleagues, caregivers, and the like. I assume they all wanted the best for me. Of course, we had altercations, no relationship is perfect. I did not mean to insult them. I had no money to gain. I think it was the obsession we shared. It must be. There is nothing else that comes to mind. We communicated often. We focused on the details of each other's lives. Daily conversations by messages, calls, and social media. I suppose it is the thing to do with someone you know. But it became a fixation. It developed into a craze to capture every moment and experience of my life. Using that knowledge to dictate my future actions and even my thoughts. I had to do something. I was overwhelmed. It became unbearable. I must admit I did something wrong to these people. Something I could not control. I had to be alone. I had to rid myself of their obsession.

Let me guess, you think this is strange. I appear mad. Insane people talk nonsense. But you did not bear witness to my actions. The measures I took were concise. The operation went smoothly only due to my attention to detail. I was alert and vigilant when I performed the deed. I have been tender and warmhearted when dealing with these intimate people in the past. Always on my best behavior. It was only a matter of time for me to erupt. And now I reside in this familiar place in agony.

You see there is no insanity. I am simply responsive to what I have done. I am in turmoil as I reflect. I see my beloved ones at this location. Their faces engraved on the walls and hearing deep breaths underneath the floor similar to a gasp of air. It upset me. I wanted to forget them.

I remained calm. However, I could not ignore the fact that this familiar place came alive. Concealing the grim fact that the residue remained of my loved ones. I heard a noise at the door. It was knocking and the annoyance of the doorbell. I checked and reluctantly acquainted the guests. It was someone I knew alongside the police. How could I have forgotten this dear person? They arrived due to some uncertain noise and the speculation of missing people. I created a vail of understanding. I greeted this familiar person with grace. I pretended to be confused of the disappearance of our mutual companions. In a placid disposition, I allowed the officer to search the area.

I became slightly agitated. The officer seemed burdened by the whole process. The real trouble was my dear loved one. It appeared as if he were here to antagonize us. I felt very weary. Worrisome and fearful. I was upset that I forgot this dear person. I regained composure as the officer felt accomplished with his exploration. There was nothing discovered. I made bizarre eye contact with my relative as we were uncomfortable with one another. There was no proof of wrongdoing. They left. I was alone in this familiar place with no person to blame but myself…

By Earvin Eugene

The diamond shines more bright than any other object. It is profound that it is created perfectly in such harsh conditions. Diamonds are forever! It is molded to be the hardest of all stones. Personally, I am lackluster in the jewel. The obsession by many is a topic of vanity. To own diamonds is self-preserved impurity. Its aligned ridges and transparent view do not motivate me. If it would be praised as some sort of tool for its unearthly qualities, there could be a discussion. "Always Diamonds" is brought to my attention. Whether for a ring for marriage or for some supreme gift to a loved one, it baffles me. "Always Diamonds" reminds me of a fierce narrative. A brutal story of unprincipled self-conceit. The draw of an enchantress combined with futility.

This myth resembles folklore. It collected plenty of notoriety. Some suggest it as the opposite with notability for the lessons it offer. A form of art to converse on literature. Thoughts on life after death became meaningful. Also, concepts of beauty are mentioned and ideas of how to label such things. And with many fables, some people believed it all to be true. Nobody is alive today to bear witness to such past events, but we can all imagine the story.

The tale takes place in North America, long before modern settlers. The land was bountiful and majestic. There were clear water rivers, green forests, and healthy animals roamed. The sky was always blue with few clouds. Sunny days were common. Mountains appeared in the distance, seeming like a mirage. The fertile land stretched on in what felt like forever. It was Manifest Destiny before people deemed it that. In the country resided a leader. He was of a royalty. His father was the leader of the land before him, and his grandfather before his father. The leader found a pretty lady to be his wife. She was elegant and kind. The two spent their time living free. Always happy without a care in the world. One forsaken day, the wife became ill. The cause was unknown. There was no real documentation of time but the myth, established that they lived healthy for a couple of years. Now the sickness and death of the wife occurred quick. A time lapse of only six months. The death was a tragedy.

The leader dealt with the loss of his wife poorly. He fasted. He was miserable. And he rarely left his chambers. The kingdom was not at ease. The subjects were worried he may even harm himself. The leader reflected and recalled how his wife appreciated diamonds. All the things reminded him of diamonds, the spas, the gardens, the palace itself. The fable even suggests that the tradition of a wife wearing a diamond ring began with the lovers. As the leader gifted his living wife a diamond ring. Only two seasons ago they embraced the palace together. The kingdom loved seeing both of them together.

Contemplation led to a decision. The leader would build a shrine for remembrance and mourning of his wife. It would be beautiful! The first task at hand was crafting the coffin. It would be of the smoothest wood with diamonds embedded on the corners and the center. It took weeks to mold the amazing coffin from idea to product. Word spread of the marvelous creations the leader was prepared to make. The followers were at awe from the finished casket alone. The leader put the cist on display. The diamonds were magnificent in the sun. This followed a speech by the leader and his staff. He proclaimed that the box would be situated in a spectacular tomb. In the coming months, the tomb was projected. It contained colorful glass windows embroidered with diamonds. At night when the moon light shined through the aperture it was a sight to see. On the walls of the tomb were drawings of moments shared between the husband and wife. It possessed the caliber of images that could be rendered by a camera. The villagers could not believe it. They wanted to pay their respects. The leader ceased their actions and stated, "Do not welcome this tomb, as it will be enclosed in a stupendous building. Then, it will be finished and we all shall embrace it." Many believed the leader was obsessed. They thought this venture was becoming ridiculous. All were afraid. Townspeople and associates would not dare bring the leader down to earth.

The construction would take a couple of years to complete. It mimicked a chapel. It was developed with pillars with custom diamonds. The layers were extravagant. From the outermost layer presenting a chapel, in the middle a tomb, and innermost a coffin. Finally, in awkward celebration, everyone said their prayers to the dead wife. Inside the coffin she rested. She was dressed in brilliant garments with a diamond ring on her finger. The entire day was dedicated for her appreciation.

Alone, in the palace, was the leader. He was not fulfilled. The chapel was created to be in perfect view from the palace. His team provided bad news that the kingdom was now in great debt. The only thing the leader could say was, "I cannot look at that monstrosity…"

By Earvin Eugene

There were once two siblings that bonded together. Their beloved mother passed. They were alone and committed to one another. Their new adopted family were brutal and harsh. They wished to stray away from them for some time. So, they decided to get some fresh air. The two walked to the park. It was a hot day. They spent the whole day searching for happiness. One moment, the brother wanted water, therefore the relatives went exploring for refreshments.

The rude stepfather would call them constantly. They were afraid. They did not want punishment. The two wanted to escape the ruthlessness of the new family. They ignored the calls of reprimand.

The siblings approached a water fountain, but the sister was determined for the brother to not drink of said fountain. She warned, "This water is dirty, brother please do not drink from this fountain." The brother accepted his sister's demands. Of course, she wanted his best interests. They walked for some time. Searching for another place to replenish their needs. The brother found a restaurant. They entered and the boy asked to buy a water bottle. The sister, stated, "The water here is too expensive. Brother please do not buy this water. We can find something better." The brother trusted his sister. He listened and they left the establishment. However, the boy mentioned, "Sister, all this movement is making me very thirsty. The next stop I must drink water." The sister agreed. Finally, the brother and sister arrived at a convenient store. The journey was far away from home. The water is cheap. The sister alerted the brother, "Please do not drink this water, it will make you sick." The brother could not listen. He was too thirsty. The boy bought the water bottle and drank the water immediately. The water tasted so good. It quit his thirst. However, he held his stomach in pain moments after. The brother began to sweat. Soon, he vomited outside the store. He was, indeed, sick.

The sister was worried for her brother. He was in pain and agony. The two could not depend on their family. If they were to go to the hospital, the two would get into more trouble. Therefore, the siblings walked further into the park. The brother coughing and vomiting along the way. The sister was protective. She said, "Do not worry brother, everything will be okay. I will take care of you."

The brother and sister relaxed at the park. They lay on the grass by a tree. She comforted her sibling. He was in fever, but she calmed him any way she could. She hoped her brother would be healed.

The boy begged his sister to find a place to relieve himself. She was worried to be separated from her brother. Nonetheless, she accepted. The brother walked away from the sister to find safety. She stated, "Please return as soon as possible." The boy guaranteed his return in due time.

The brother expelled his disease. He would feel slightly better with each expulsion. As soon as he felt better, he would return to the girl. However, the next few days the cycle would continue in this manner. He would leave to the privacy to remove his infection and return to his beloved sister. She prayed that this would end.

The sister noticed the brother started expelling blood. She was aware of the blood on his clothing. She knew the expulsions was not the answer. The sister exclaimed, "One day you will wish to relieve yourself and not return. Brother you are dying! We must do something."

The brother stated, "I will die if I stay with you and not expel my disease. When the urge comes upon me, I must release this trouble." The sister reluctantly agreed. The next day when the boy left to deal with his sickness, a gentleman arrived at the park. It has been days since the siblings been with their ruthless family. She was fearful. The gentleman found the girl intriguing. The man stated, "What are you doing alone at the park? You should not stay here alone. She said, "I am with my brother and he is sick, we need help. Will you provide help?" The gentleman guaranteed support. He mentioned, "When you brother comes back, we will treat him." The sister was skeptical. She only offered partnership for the sake of her brother.

As the brother and sister was greeted and treated by the gentleman, they were ecstatic. The man not only provided medical relief for the brother but provided housing for the siblings. Once the stepfather and troublesome family heard notice, they were angry. The family wanted misfortune for the siblings.

The merciless family sent an intruder to the residence of the gentleman and the siblings. The intruder demanded the return of the siblings. The gentleman heard stories of the cruel family from the girl and did not trust the presence of the intruder. The man, stated, "You should leave at once! I am taking care of these two siblings. Your involvement is not necessary." The man protected the siblings.

The intruder was repelled, and safety was established to the brother and sister. As time went on the brother and sister lived a healthy life. The brother was restored. Everything was at peace.

By Earvin Eugene

Outside the grass was green. People were shopping around at a garage sale. There were some precious mementos and some boring objects. The thing that caught the eye of one particular shopper was a pair of shoes. They were black and white sneakers. It appeared to be a set of typical everyday sneakers. It was the perfect size for him. He asked the seller, "How much for those shoes?" The man replied, "These are strange shoes. I have owned them for years. The last person that bought these shoes, returned them to me. How much are you willing to pay?" The guy stated, "How about twenty dollars? I really need some shoes. Plus, they look vintage!" The man responded, "Let's settle at twenty-two dollars." The guy accepted the deal.

The guy returned home with his new sneakers. He decided to test them out by playing basketball with his friends. He changed outfits and put on his gear. He matched his basketball shorts with the sneakers. The guy felt confident and ready to play. His friends arrived and waited outside to play on his driveway. They took several shots and rejoiced when the guy came outside his house to join them. One friend notified him that a package arrived. He was confused because he was not expecting any deliveries. He left the parcel on his steps. He would tend to it later, after playing two versus two basketball with his friends. There was friendly competition between the players.

After calling plays, running around, lay ups, and shooting they were exhausted. The guy invited his friends inside for refreshments. They discussed about the game to be on television tonight. They were not going to spend the night as they had to return to other things. They were going to shower and watch the game with their girlfriends. The guy was single and liked it that way, at least for now. He was focused on the package. He thought to himself, "What could it be?" The friends noticed him staring at the package during conversation. One pal suggested, "Dude, just open the package!" Another friend mentioned, "It could be from that new girl, you are talking to." The guy decided to open the package. It was a pair of white socks. He was astonished. His friend said, "The socks match your new sneakers!" The guy replied, "You are right" One pal stated, "Where is the package from?" The guy checked the address, it appeared the package was from Maine. The guy stated, "I do not know anyone from Maine?" The other friend said, "Just be happy that you got a free gift." All the friends conversed on current events for a short period of time. "Nobody ever goes to malls or shops in-person anymore. Everything is delivered to homes. I think social distancing will make people more cold. People are so awkward when greeted nowadays." The friends agreed. One pal, stated "You pay for convenience." It was getting late. It was dark outside now. They left. The guy was alone with his thoughts. To stay busy, he watched television and made food. He showered after the game. He prepared for bed and wore the new socks.

In the coming days, the guy performed errands and continued with his normal routine. He went for a drive and walked into a coffee shop in the town. In the city, he viewed the cars passing by and the citizens walking on the sidewalks. What caught his eye was mailman vehicle. The postman looked familiar. He waved hello to the guy with a smile. The guy found this peculiar but returned the gesture. The delivery man was far away, across the street. At that moment there plenty of traffic. The guy continued with his day. The guy was on the phone with his older brother, as he sat outside a café. They talked about their family. He mentioned the fact that he received a package from Maine. The brother found this weird. The brother reminded him that he was going to visit him in a few days. They said their salutations. The guy returned home. He received an unknown number call. The voice was creepy. It said, "You got mail coming to you…" The guy was upset. He did not like someone playing a prank on him. He calmed his nerves by listening to some music. He used his headphones and went to bed.

Several days passed. Each day he angrily waited for the mail. Everyday it was regular mail. Today, there was a package! The guy quickly saw where it was from. The parcel stated it was from Arizona. The guy thought, I do not know anyone from Arizona. He stared at the package with vexation. He received a phone

call. Before answering, he was irritated. He thought it would be an unknown caller.
The guy checked the phone and it was his brother. The brother said, "Are you
home?" He replied, "Yeah, I received another package! This time it is from
Arizona." The brother said, "Do not open the package yet, I am on my way. We'll
open it together and get to the bottom of this." They agreed.

The guy questioned the purpose of these packages. The brothers opened the
package. It was sweatpants! They were confused. The sweatpants matched the
socks, and the sneakers. The guy noticed this, as he wore the socks and shoes. The
brother not taking the matter seriously said, "Try on the sweatpants." The guy,
replied, "That is not funny". The brother stated, "Did you see who delivered the
package?" The guy said, "I suppose it was the mailman? Who else could it be?"
The brother brought something important to his sibling's attention. "You never
paid attention to who has been dropping off your packages?" The guy stated, "No."
The older brother established a plan. He said, "Next time you get any package, see
who delivers it. Plant a camera on the front door." The brothers agreed.

The guy was surfing the internet on a particular evening. He was playing
games online. He took a moment to order a book from a website. Suddenly, after
the purchase he heard strange sounds in his backyard. The guy explored the
premises. Nothing was found. He texted one of his friends to find comfort. There
was no answer. For a minute, he relaxed in his room. Then, he went to use the

bathroom. As soon as he finished, there was a similar weird sound again. This time, it appeared to come from the front of the house. He remembered the front door camera. The guy went to view the feedback of the camera on his computer. He noticed a silhouette approaching the front of the house. The guy grabbed a household weapon, a simple table knife to protect himself. He was agitated and anxious. He could not decipher the true identity of the person approaching. To make matters worse, he abruptly heard the notification from his cellphone. He thought to himself now or never. He slightly concealed the weapon and opened the front door and yelled "Who is that?" A great sense of relief came onto him as he heard a familiar, "What's going on bro?" It was his brother. He brought food and drinks for the last night of his stay. The guy said, "You scared me!" The brother entered the house with groceries and stated, "This is not healthy for you. These packages are getting to your head." The guy was calm now. He checked his phone. The notification was a text message from his friend saying, "Are you okay?" The guy believed he was becoming paranoid. He thought he was becoming a burden to his family and friends. The brothers enjoyed the last evening together, eating and watching videos online.

A few days passed. The guy received a notification that his book was to arrive today. He was glad. It was during the day. The guy invited his friend. She recommended the book to him. They were planning to enjoy the book together. A package arrived. They assumed it was the book. It was a package from New Mexico. The guy was upset. He said, "Not again!" The girl stated, "What is wrong?" The guy described the situation. The girl believed it was not a big issue. She believed he was overreacting. She said, "I would not mind receiving free stuff. Let us see what it is." The guy reluctantly opened the package. Now the gift was a blank T-shirt. She said, "I do not know if I like it, but it is free. Try it on." The shirt fit him perfectly. The girl inquired, "What else did you receive?" The guy showed her the socks and sweatpants. She was curious. The girl said, "Do you realize it all matches?" The guy sadly agreed. She suggested he try all the gifts at once. The girl said, "Make it a new outfit!" The guy wore the socks, the sweatpants, and the new shirt. The guy said, "Oh I forgot, I bought these classic sneakers! Now that I think of it, it goes along with the outfit." She said, "Put it on!" The guy wore everything. She said, "Cool, but it is missing something." The guy was clueless. He replied, "I don't know?" She said, "I don't know either. Let me think about it." Soon, another package arrived. It was the book. The guy found easement knowing it was simply the book. They went to the backyard and discussed the book. It was fun and relaxing.

After a few hours, the girl was excited. She said, "You're missing a hat! That's what would make your outfit perfect." The guy wanted to connect with the girl, so he agreed. They spent time entertaining one another. Time flies when you are having fun. It was nighttime now. It was time for the girl to leave. She kissed him goodbye and said, "I will buy you a matching hat!" The guy replied, "I look forward to it. Thank you." She went on her way.

Several days passed by. It was the guy's day off. There was not much to do. He would just amuse himself. The whole day went by slow. It was a boring day. It was quiet before the storm. He looked in the mirror. By some strange luck, he was wearing that same intriguing outfit. The guy did not pay much attention to fashion. He heard the doorbell ring. The guy looked around, it appeared to be typical day in the neighborhood. At his doorstep was a package! It was from Georgia. He showed no emotion to the predicament. He placed the package on the counter. The guy thought it is probably a hat. He realized it was, indeed, a hat! Of course, it matched the outfit. Instead of getting angry, he recalled the girl was planning to buy him a hat. The thing that puzzled him was, why Georgia? He did not obsess about it. Perhaps the hat company or some shipping factory resided in Georgia. He texted the girl and said, "Thanks for the hat" with a photo of him wearing the matching outfit. There was no immediate response. He thought nothing of it. The guy went on with his day.

It was night now. Pitch dark. Someone broke into the house. The guy heard a notification on his phone. There was no time to pay attention to that. He fought the intruder. It was of no use. The guy was murdered. He was in the dark with that matching outfit.

END

By Earvin Eugene

Jackson attended a military preparatory academy. He bonded with the other soldiers. Training together, eating together, and simply serving together. They all were decorated in uniform. He enlisted in the Afghanistan War in 2001 and did not return to the United States until the third legion returned from the Middle East in the Summer of 2003.

There are snapshots which show him in the mountains with other soldiers. They are rugged in their uniforms. Covered by sand and dirt. The setting appears to naturally captivating to the eyes, but no sane person would want to be there long. Views of a silent dessert and sierra are deceiving.

In due time Jackson returned to his home town of San Diego. He received mixed reviews. Some people were patriots and accepted the war. They thought it necessary especially after 9/11. The war on terror was in high pursuit. Others deemed it as another excuse to invade and attack countries. Some people believed it was the chase for natural resources. At this time there was no definitive answer.

To tell the truth, Jackson exaggerated accounts of the war. One lie led to another lie. He wanted to emerge righteous but the war like many grand ventures is filled with mundane and regulated operations. Creating plans for every movement with little excursion. Checking gear for the proper use of tools. Timed training and preparing for combat. Staying hydrated in a hot environment. Providing nourishment with basic food at the same time every day. Nobody would be excited by such a boring routine. The only intriguing thing was firing the best military weapons. So, he stuck to his guns and paltered about the whole experience. Stories of firing guns against enemies. Roaming the entire country wreaking havoc from village to village. In reality, it was dangerous social work.

There was no charade in the company of other soldiers. All the fake confidence would disappear. Knowing there were moments when his life was on the line. Confronted with unseeable bombs and vicious insurgents who wanted you removed from their land. Being in an unknown land pitied with harsh conditions. Always sweating and aching with pain from carrying heavy equipment weight. Always looking over your shoulder. Sleeping with one eye open. Attempting to communicate with strangers who spoke a foreign language and not knowing who a true enemy or ally was. The loss of comrades who shared this treacherous world. There was an unspoken connection between other soldiers. The life of a soldier is demanding and tiresome. No time or place to quiver. One must assimilate to the typical life of American society, while engrained with a soldier mentality. The stress and trauma experienced are not normal. Jackson must admit to himself, at all times he was on edge.

At this moment, it was late summer, he was relaxing in bed, waking up to walk down to the park, eating lunch at home, smoking a cigarette on the front porch until he became weary and then driving through the city to drink at a shabby bar. He loved to play darts.

In the evening he played piano, in the backyard he would swim, read, and went to bed. He was still a hero to his younger brother. His mother would cook dinner for him if he pleased. She would on occasion ask him about the war, but it was a world unknown to her. His father had no opinion on the matter.

The children in the neighborhood were now grown up. Jackson remembered leaving when they knew no better. Now they were confident following their own paths. Dressing in whatever, they pleased. Wearing sweatshirts, leggings, designed T-shirts, and sneakers. He imagined they would be preparing to go to college. Partying this summer after years of school at home.

Jackson sometimes thought of girls, but he did not want to put in the effort. To pretend to be interested, to spend time doing things he did not really enjoy, and to continue to lie to impress someone. The military taught him you do not need a girl unless you thought of one. And if you really wanted one, someone that matched your preferences, in due time it would be provided. In life if you set goals and commit to a certain thing, what you seek will come to you. Some military guys wanted a girl every night. Others had no use for girls. It all depended on if you thought about it or not.

It was time for Jackson to get a job. Military service provides a lot of skills.

He just wanted life to run smoothly. So, he looked for jobs. Now, he would drive

into town. Staring at the water. Walking in the park. Watching people play

sports…